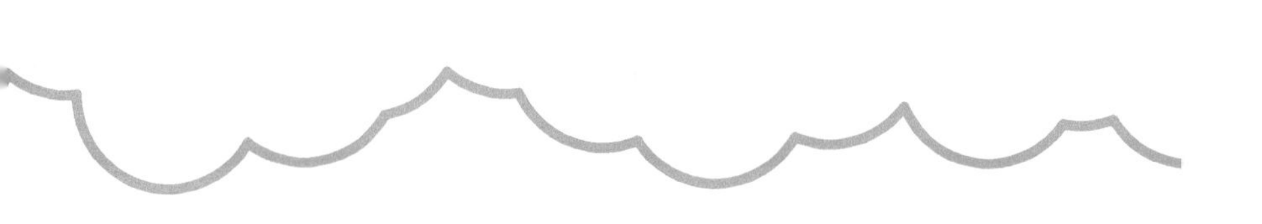

MW00884981

# The Great Zodiac Race

W C Jefferson    T F Wister

TOUCAN PUBLISHING

Long time ago, in a far away land,
A great race was held that was ever so grand.

The first twelve creatures to cross the line,
Would get their very own zodiac sign.

Everyone joined,

all hoping to win,

Now here's the story, let us begin.

The race to victory was tough and long,
It challenged all to be smart and strong.
Through mountains tall and terrain extreme,

Would the fastest win?

Or the bravest one?

Into the dark forest,

and across the stream.

Those who can fly?

Or those who can run?

Coming in first was Riley the Rat,
Against all odds, she achieved all that.
With a wooden raft she crossed the stream,

# "OH! I WON!"

Riley happily screamed.

1st

So the clever Rat,
she claimed first place,
Beating everyone
in this great long race.

Coming in next was a calm gentle soul,
Ollie knew to win was a tough tough goal.

He gave it his all, and tried his best,
It has always helped him pass any test!

FINISH
2nd

So Ollie the Ox
came in second place,
As he boldly finished
in this great race.

Zooming in fast, there was a quick dash,
It jumped in the water and made a big splash.

3rd

**TAZZIE**

**THE TIGER,**

the king of
all creatures!

Who has black stripes as his very best features?

But even the best don't always win,

Content with third place,

Tazzie smiled with a grin.

Rosie the Rabbit was close behind,

She had a winning frame of mind.

She found some rocks to cross the stream,

Faster and faster as she picked up steam!

4th

Rosie the Rabbit finished
in fourth place,
Delighted that she joined
in this fun race.

From the sky came thunder and mighty gales,
Down flew a dragon with shiny red scales.
He'd been on a mission in the far far east,
Duncan the Dragon was a gracious beast.

Proud and honored to receive fifth place,
Duncan was thankful he completed this race.

5th

On the riverbank sat Sammi the Snake,
Finding a log was her lucky break.
She floated across to the finish line,

"What place did I get for
my zodiac sign?"
6th

Happy to know she had earned sixth place,
Sammi was relieved to have finished this race.

Then a horse came galloping in,

He ran so fast he was sure to win!

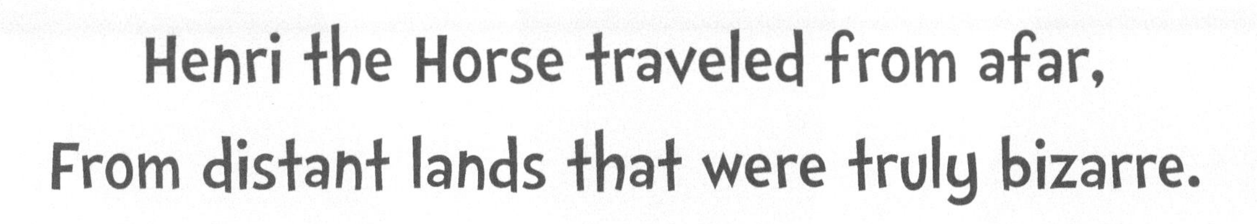

Henri the Horse traveled from afar,
From distant lands that were truly bizarre.

7th

The tired horse
claimed seventh place,

He needed a rest after his long race.

FINISH
8th

Sylvie the Sheep
accepted eighth
with grace.

Three friends later washed ashore,

In a raft like the one that was used before.

Maxi the Monkey

rejoiced with

ninth place.

9th

10th

Rocky the Rooster

was last among friends,

He was just glad to

be tenth in the end.

No one showed up for quite awhile,

Until the Dog came in with a smile.

FINISH

11th

He was playing games
while having some fun,
Then he recalled there
was a race to run.

Dylan the Dog
earned eleventh place,
Happy to achieve
a place in the race.

Only one spot left in the zodiac,
It's the final push,
there's no holding back.

Racing and running and
sprinting ahead...

Why is Josie the Cat still sleeping in bed?!

"Wake up, Josie! Get up, Cat"

"No time to sleep! No time to chat!"

Josie jumped when she heard the noise,

"Who's calling me!"

"Who's behind that voice?"

"Hello, it's me!
Reading about you!

Now go get up and
put on your shoes!"

The Cat ran quickly,
her sprinting was fast,
She was trying her best
not to be last.

She came to the river and surveyed the scene.

Josie couldn't swim, so what did this mean?

Then something moved from behind the log...

Was it a crocodile?

Was it a frog?

FINISH

It had a curly tail,
this pink old chap,
Paolo the Pig was waking
from his nap!

Paolo saw Josie,
and without a word,
A splash was the last thing
that was heard.

He was trying hard to finish the race!
Paolo wanted the last zodiac place!

Josie knew her swimming was not so good...
"I'll float across on this piece of wood!"

Paolo swam and with a final burst,

He left the water and onto land first.

Across the finish,
he claimed twelfth place,
The Pig was done with
this challenging race.

FINISH

Still in the water,
Josie knew she lost,
Waking up late was a very big cost.

Josie the Cat came in thirteenth place,
The others still cheered as she finished the race.

At the same time, she felt mad and sad,
Then she explained why she felt so bad:

FINISH

"Sometimes you win,
Sometimes you lose,
Sometimes it's luck,
But often it's what you choose."

2020
1936
1948
1960
1972
1984
1996
2008

2021
1937
1949
1961
1973
1985
1997
2009

2022
1938
1974
1986
1998
2010

Each year of our birth has a zodiac sign,
She is a sheep, and the horse is mine.
Others can guess your age for sure,
By knowing the animal sign of yours.

2026
1942
1954
1966
1978
1990
2002
2014

2027
1943
1955
1967
1979
1991
2003
2015

2028
1944
1956
1968
1980
1992
2004
2016

1939
1951
1963
1975
1987
1999
2011
2023

1940
1952
1964
1976
1988
2000
2012
2024

1941
1953
1965
1977
1989
2001
2013
2025

But those of you
who want to hide your age,
Say you're a "Cat,"
then it's hard to gauge!

1945
1957
1969
1981
1993
2005
2017
2029

1946
1958
1970
1982
1994
2006
2018
2030

1947
1959
1971
1983
1995
2007
2019
2031

“ For Jo, Joshua and Jayden ”

W.C.J.

This book is the labor of love started from a dream: W C Jefferson and T F Wister, thank you - for your passion, tenacity and unwavering dedication.

Published by Toucan Publishing

ISBN: 978-988-78009-0-3



Check out all book titles at **www.13zodiac.com**

CPSIA information can be obtained
at www.ICGtesting.com
Printed in the USA
LVHW071027010419
612303LV00025B/112/P